2004-2005

Fairlawn ELC fundraising has donated this book to proudly acknowledge first grader.

Alyssa   Raheb

a reader and life-long learner.

The Paper Princess Finds Her Way

ELISA KLEVEN

Dutton Children's Books • New York

Library of Congress Cataloging-in-Publication Data

Kleven, Elisa.
  The paper princess finds her way/by Elisa Kleven.—1st ed.
    p.   cm.
  Sequel to: The paper princess.
  Summary: After the girl who drew her grows older and no longer plays
with her, a paper princess lets the wind carry her off to adventures which
include a cat, a Christmas tree, butterflies, and a new home.
  ISBN 0-525-46911-7
  [1. Princesses—Fiction. 2. Drawing—Fiction. 3. Toys—Fiction.]
I. Title.
PZ7.K6783875Par 2003
[E]—dc21   2002041410

Published in the United States 2003 by Dutton Children's Books,
a division of Penguin Young Readers Group
345 Hudson Street, New York, New York 10014
www.penguin.com

Manufactured in China • Designed by Tim Hall
First Edition
3 5 7 9 10 8 6 4 2

With love to Dad and Sally

A paper princess lived a good life with the little girl who had made her. She wore a dress like a forest, starry socks, and watermelon shoes. She rode a paper elephant, and played with a paper brother, and flew along when the little girl rode her bike. And whenever she needed a new crown, the girl would make her one.

But as the little girl grew up, she played less with her paper toys. One day, she left the elephant outside, and he blew away. Another time, she used the paper brother as a bookmark and forgot to take him out when she returned the book to the library.

"I'd better keep my princess safe," said the girl, sitting the princess up on her dresser beneath a paperweight.

Day after day, the princess sat. The sun beat down on her, fading her clothes (but not her friendly face, which was drawn in ink).

"Do you think you could draw me a new dress?" the princess asked the girl one day. "And could you take me for a ride like you used to?"

But the girl didn't answer.

"Why doesn't she talk to me anymore?" the princess asked the girl's old dog.

"She's changing," the dog said. "Children stop hearing their toys when they grow up. She wants to go out and make new friends."

"I wish I could go out and make new friends," said the princess. "I wish I could change."

"You're just a little paper doll," the dog replied. "You might not change for the best out there. It can be a hard world for small, fragile things."

"It can't be much harder than sitting in here, fading away like an old piece of homework."

The princess sounded so sad that the dog wanted to help her. He nudged the paperweight aside with his nose,

took her gently in his mouth, and carried her outdoors to freedom.

The dog watched the wind whisk her off. "Good luck out there. I hope you find your way."

"Thanks, dear dog!" the princess called, turning cartwheels as she went.

The princess hadn't gone far when a cat spotted her skittering down the sidewalk like a mouse. He chased her, and batted her with his paws, and tore off her crown, and smiled a sharp cat smile.

I must keep my head about me, thought the princess, trying to see some way out of her fix.

Not far away, the princess spotted a baby throwing fistfuls of fish-shaped crackers. "Look, cat!" she cried. "Fish, right over there! Tasty, golden fish, waiting just for you."

"Fish?" The cat trotted off to investigate, dropping the princess at the baby's feet.

The baby grabbed the princess in her chubby hands. "Jink!" she told the princess, giving her some cranberry juice.

"Umm," said the princess. "Delicious!"

The baby laughed and shook her bottle, spattering juice on the princess's dress.

The princess laughed, too. "Well, that's one way to change my dress."

"Candy!" the baby gurgled, popping the princess into her mouth.

"NO!" yelled the princess. "NOT candy!"

"NO!" said the baby's father. "No yucky papers in your mouth!"

"Mine!" screamed the baby.

The father eyed the princess. "Oh, it's a paper doll," he said. "What a nice, hand-drawn face she has. I know—we'll put her inside with your special toys and save her till you're bigger."

The father set the princess high on a shelf crowded with brand-new toys.

"Heavens!" cried a queen doll with a jeweled crown. "Why did the gentleman leave litter on our shelf?"

"I'm not litter," said the princess. "I'm a princess. I had a crown, but a cat tore it off. And I had a beautiful dress but it faded, and the baby splashed juice on me."

"Some princess," sniffed the queen. "You look more like a drippy old Popsicle wrapper. What store did you come from, anyway?"

"No store," said the princess. "A little girl made me."

The toys all stared at her. "A little girl *made* you?"

"So you're not from a catalog, then?" asked a wind-up ballerina.

"No, a little girl drew me and cut me out. Haven't you ever heard of paper dolls?"

"*Paper* dolls?" demanded the queen. "Who would want to own a paper doll? What can a paper doll do?"

"They don't have any wind-up keys to help them twirl around," remarked the ballerina.

"Or batteries to make them go," a fiery race car added.

"Or computer chips," said a bear-shaped computer, "to help them do math and spell words! Indeed, what can a paper doll do?"

"I can play," said the princess. "I can make the baby laugh."

A sudden wind gusted through the window, twirling the princess around. "I can dance!"

"I can fly!" she sang as the wind lifted her right out the window.

"She can fly!" gasped the toys. "Without any computer chips! Or wind-up keys! Or batteries!" Even the queen was impressed. "She can fly all by herself!"

Well, almost, thought the princess. I just need some help from the wind. I wish the wind would take me flying all around the world!

But the wind had other ideas. Slowly, it let the princess drop

 down,

down,

 down.

A boy saw her falling softly as snow.

"An angel!" he said, catching her. "With a Christmasy red and green dress. Just what we need."

The princess was too excited to speak. An angel? Just what they need? She trembled in the boy's cupped hands.

When the boy opened his hands, the princess found herself on a table, surrounded by markers and glitter and glue and pieces of paper and cloth. Oh! she thought. Just like my girl's table used to look. I wonder what he's going to make?

"Wings," said the boy. "That's all she needs." He cut some scraps of silk into a glowing pair of wings and glued them to the princess's back.

"Look, Mom," he told his mother, "an angel for the top of the Christmas tree. She's not as fancy as our old glass angel was—"

"But she's not as fragile, either," said his mother. "For now she'll do just fine."

What could be finer than being at the top of the Christmas tree? thought the princess.

I feel like I have a great, green, sweet-smelling dress . . .

and they're decorating my dress with candy canes and shiny balls and popcorn and bells . . .

and they're dancing all around me and singing. . . . I wish they would
sing forever!

Soon the house grew quiet, though, and one morning the boy's mother began picking the ornaments off the tree. "What happens now?" the princess asked her neighbor, the wooden nutcracker.

"What always happens," the nutcracker replied. "We get packed away in boxes for another year."

"Ugh," said the princess. "I'll hate being packed away."

"Not to worry, then," said the nutcracker. "Only the good ornaments get packed. The paper ones like you get tossed outdoors with the tree."

"Well, I'd rather be outdoors than packed," said the princess. "I'm glad I'm paper."

And she was glad, for the air outdoors was fresh and crisp, and around her the winter birds chirped.

But the next day a storm blustered out of the sky, knocking down the Christmas tree, trapping the princess in a tangle of branches. Rain fell, and she huddled beneath her silk wings. Snow fell, and she sank into a deep, frozen sleep.

Spring came, waking the earth, and the princess with it. Her dress
was just a tatter, but her wings were bright as ever, and her spirit stirred
at the sight of blossoms and soft blue sky.

How good it is to be even a tiny scrap of the springtime world, she
thought. Now, if only I could fly away from this dry old tree. "Anybody
there?" she called in her paper-thin voice. But nobody heard her . . .

and nobody came, day after day, not even the wind.

The old dog was right, thought the princess one late-summer day. It's a hard world for small, fragile things. She sang a song to break the quietness around her:

The leaves are flying like tiny kites,
The clouds are tumbling, fluffy and white,
The sun's a gold ball in a playground of blue,
But I'm stuck in this tree like glue.

"Let's get you out, then," said a small voice. "Come, sister, it's time to go."

The princess looked up and saw a handsome orange and black butterfly. "Don't get left behind now," it said. "Winter will soon come again."

"But I can't fly as well as you," said the princess. "My wings are only cloth."

Another butterfly, and another, and more fluttered around her. "We'll lift you," they said. "We'll help you glide on the wind with us. You can sing to us as we make our long journey." Together the butterflies pushed aside the tree's brittle branches . . .

and carried the princess up on a cloud of wings.
"Hooray!" yelled the princess. "I'm flying again."

"Where are we flying to?" she asked.

"To a warm country, far far away," said a butterfly. "Where we won't fear the cold or the snow."

"You're so small to travel so far," said the princess as they coasted above a steep cliff. "How do you find your way?"

"We just do," the butterflies answered. "The same as our relatives who have gone before us. The same way we know how to change from caterpillars to butterflies."

"I changed from a paper doll to an angel to a kind of butterfly," said the princess.

"Bravo!" said the butterflies.

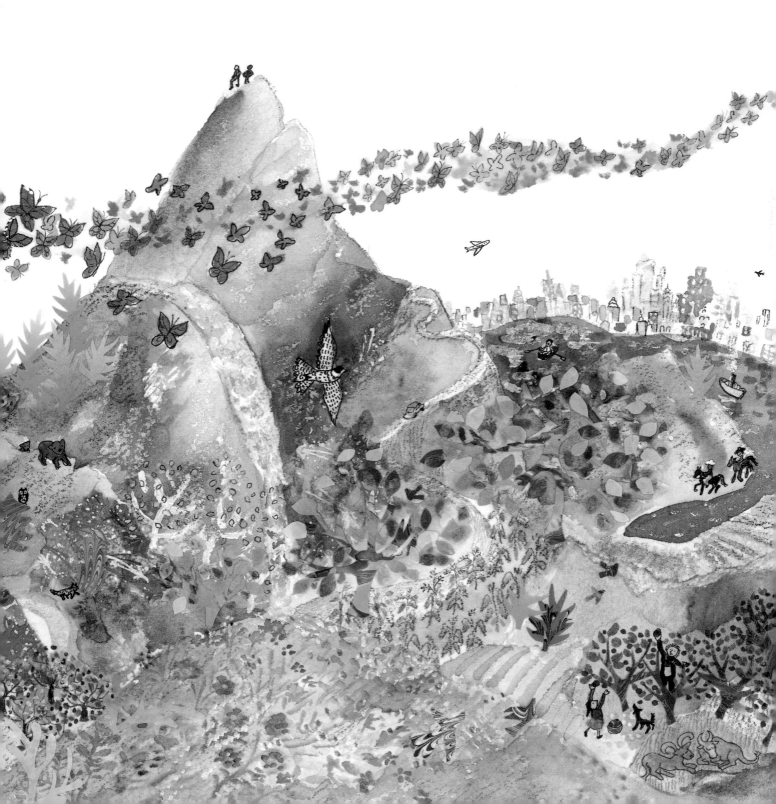

Together they traveled, a magic carpet of sunlit wings, over cities and rivers, valleys and clouds.

Each evening, when the sun went down, they stopped to rest in trees; each morning, when it rose, they forged on, fortified by the princess's songs. At last they reached the warm country.

"Hooray!" the people greeted them. "The butterflies are back!"
Children, dressed like butterflies, sang and drummed and danced.
They clapped, and flapped their painted wings, and the butterflies
flapped, too.

And in all the excitement, the princess tumbled

down,

down,

down.

A little girl picked her up. "Poor butterfly, your wings must be broken . . . and you have a face . . . and a bit of a dress. What kind of butterfly are you?"

"I'm a princess-angel-butterfly," the princess replied.

"You are?" asked the girl. "Where did you come from?"

"I came from another little girl, who grew up," the princess began. "I've been in the claws of a cat and the mouth of a baby; on a shelf with fancy toys and at the top of a Christmas tree; under winter snows and over autumn mountainsides. I've traveled so far, and I've changed again and again."

"Would you like a change of clothes?" the girl asked. "I could make you a new princess dress while you tell me about your adventures."

"I'd love that," said the princess.

While the princess told her stories, the girl made her a dress like the
sky, rainbow socks, strawberry shoes, a flowery crown . . .

a paper dog to play with, and a soft mossy bed to sleep in each night.

The princess was very happy.

She knew she had found her way.